What Does "Depressed" Mean?

A Guidebook for Children with a Depressed Loved One

Written by Therese J. Borchard

Illustrated by R.W. Alley

ONE
CARING
PLACE

Abbey Press
St. Meinrad, IN 47577

Dedication:

For my children, David and Katherine—
May this help you to better understand your mom.

Text © 2011 Therese Borchard
Illustrations © 2011 Saint Meinrad Archabbey
Published by One Caring Place
Abbey Press
St. Meinrad, Indiana 47577

Library of Congress Catalog Number
2011937782

ISBN 978-0-87029-469-3

Printed in the United States of America.

A Message to Parents, Teachers, and Other Caring Adults

In any given year, about one in four Americans develops at least one mental health disorder, according to a national survey. In 2007, 16.5 million American adults—close to eight percent of the population—suffered at least one episode of major depression, and fewer than two-thirds (65%) received treatment. A considerable number of these are parents, grandparents, or primary caregivers of young children. When the adults fail to meet the needs of the little people under their care, some kids begin to act out, have difficulty with schoolwork, and become hyperactive. A sizable percentage of children start to isolate and feel depressed themselves.

Unfortunately, adult depression never happens in a vacuum. It has a ripple effect that can leave the child confused, angry, sad … wondering why the mother that used to read her bedtime stories at night and tickle her until she screamed "Stop!" now doesn't tuck her in at all; or baffled as to why Dad no longer takes her on Saturday morning errands, which she had always looked forward to.

Depression is unlike a cancer diagnosis in that it is so elusive and individualized. Although major depression often includes telltale symptoms like fatigue, no appetite, loss of interest in hobbies, sleeping difficulty, isolation, and so on, it can be much harder to explain to a child than an illness that requires insulin or chemotherapy. The depressed person looks perfectly normal on the outside, so it is hard to appreciate the pain that goes on inside.

This book is an attempt to explain depression to children in language they can understand. It is my hope that with a little better understanding of the depression of a parent, grandparent, or caregiver, a child will be less afraid and more patient for the return of the healthy and nurturing loved one.

—*Therese Borchard*

Your Loved One Is Sick

You have probably heard someone say that your loved one is "depressed," and you wonder what that means. You understand when a friend breaks his leg, or sprains a wrist, or has the flu. But what does it mean when someone's depressed?

Depression is an illness like any other illness. The messengers inside the brain that deliver notes from one side to the other get stuck ... kind of like when you are supposed to bring in a permission slip from a parent to your teacher. If the note never got there, your teacher wouldn't know what to do, right? Depression is the same sort of thing. Messages get stuck, and so the person becomes confused or sad.

Depression Is Invisible

Depression is very weird because it's invisible!
It's like the hidden pictures in those 3-D posters.
Unless you wear 3-D glasses, you can't see them.
In the same way, your loved one looks perfectly
normal, right? It's hard to believe that he or she
is sick.

Try to imagine the depression like the hidden
pictures in a poster. What you see on the outside
isn't all that is there. It isn't like looking at an
apple and knowing that it is an apple. You can't see
depression with your eyes, but it is still a sickness
that needs to be treated.

You Are Not to Blame

When I was a little girl, my mom was depressed and I used to think it was my fault … that she was sad because I wasn't as good or as smart as she wanted me to be, or that she was disappointed by something that I had said or done. I was sure that I had upset her, but I didn't know what I did. That wasn't true at all! She told me so after she felt better.

It is easy to blame yourself when someone is depressed, but the illness has nothing to do with you!

It's Okay to Cry

Did you know that crying is good for you? Like eating a big piece of broccoli or a fresh apple? When you cry, the icky stuff that gets stuck somewhere in your body comes out with your tears! It's like taking a bath. But instead of cleaning up your outside, it cleans your insides.

Crying is a wonderful way of expressing your sadness, and being sad about somebody's depression is normal and good. Something would be wrong if you weren't sad and never cried. You would get all dirty inside!

Don't Take It Personally

Sometimes depressed people say things they don't mean. It's like when your teacher doesn't want you to use certain words. You do a pretty good job of that, but then you have a day here and there when you say the words anyway!

When people are depressed, they say the words they aren't supposed to say. But they don't have a teacher to tell them not to say them anymore. They are frustrated because they feel bad, so sometimes they scream at someone just because the person is in the same room! Try not to take it personally. The depressed person is just mad because they don't feel good.

You Are Still Loved

When a person is grumpy, it is easy to think that he or she no longer loves you. Their actions—tears, yelling, grumpy fits—speak louder than their words. It's hard to remember they still love you even when they are not acting like they do.

Imagine if someone was pinching you and wouldn't let go. Then your friend comes over and wants to ride bikes down the street. You might say, "No! Go away! I am being pinched!" It's not that you don't like or love your friend, but you are uncomfortable because of the pinching.

You are still very much loved by the person who is depressed.

Depression Is Treatable

The very good news about depression is that it can easily be treated! Unlike other illnesses where there is a high chance that the person will never get better, most people who are depressed soon feel better.

They may need a few weeks, or maybe even a few months, to take medicine and do other things they need to do to feel better, but it won't be long before they have as much energy as they did before. There is hope! Lots of hope!

Try to Be Patient

It can be very hard to be patient when someone we love feels bad. We want to make their illness go away quickly, to help them in some way, so things can get back to normal.

Having patience is one of the hardest parts of having someone we love suffer from depression. When my mom got depressed, I tried not to think about when she would get better. Someone told me to take each day as it came, and to try to concentrate on me, doing the things that I could do for myself.

Ask for Help

Did you know that some of the strongest people in the history of our country didn't try to do things by themselves? I'm thinking of Abraham Lincoln and George Washington, and most of our presidents! Instead, they asked for help and lots of it.

Asking for help is not a sign of weakness. It is a sign of strength. Because we all need help from time to time with something or another. And even when you grow up, you don't stop asking for help. I ask for help everyday!

Rely on Others

When I was in grade school, I didn't like group projects because you had to rely on other people, and I wanted to control everything. Sometimes I would do the whole project by myself. I would get really tired, and the other people would get mad, and the teacher was not happy!

Living with someone who is depressed is like a group project. Everybody has to work together so that no one gets too tired. Maybe someone makes sure that the depressed person is eating good foods. Someone might handle all the doctor's appointments. It is important that you rely on others for help during this time, too.

Your Loved One Will Be Back

It is hard to imagine that the person who is now depressed will one day be back to herself. It is scary when you think that she might be sad for the rest of her life.

However, you must trust that the same person who read bedtime stories to you, or tickled you until you screamed "Stop!" or took you on Saturday morning errands will be back! For real!

Do Something You Enjoy

Here's an easy way to let time pass until your loved one is feeling better: do something that you like to do! Not only will it make you happier, but you will forget about your loved one's depression for a little bit of time.

It is actually very healthy for your brain to have these kinds of moments where you can forget about the problems at home and focus on you. It's like letting your brain to take a nap for awhile…and it can get very tired when it's worried about a loved one.

Talk About It

I know it can be scary to open your heart to people and tell them about your feelings. But, just like crying, talking about what is bothering you almost always makes you feel better. It's a little like pulling dead weeds so that new flowers can grow.

Most of the time, when you share your sadness with someone, you find out that you are not alone, and that many other people have the same type of sadness. Sometimes they can give you ideas that helped them to feel better. Wonderful things happen when you share your pain.

Depend on God

You are so lucky. You have a Heavenly Father that is watching over you every single minute. The Bible is full of verses that tell us so! Scripture says that our Father knows every hair on our heads and every thought in our hearts…and during the moments we are most sad or scared, God will actually carry us!

Depend on God, because his love is always there … in times of sadness and in joy. God can give you a feeling of peace in your heart even when things aren't just right at home.

Therese J. Borchard is the author of *Beyond Blue: Surviving Depression & Anxiety and Making the Most of Bad Genes*. She lives in Annapolis, Maryland, with her husband and two children, and can be found at www.thereseborchard.com.

R. W. Alley is the illustrator for the popular Abbey Press adult series of Elf-help books, as well as an illustrator and writer of children's books. He lives in Barrington, Rhode Island, with his wife, daughter, and son. See a wide variety of his works at: www.rwalley.com.